ABCD ~ The Rhythm Of Life

Book*Squirrel* Publication

Regd. Under MSME Act.

" <u>**ABCD – The Rhythm of Life**</u> "

By: Twisha Ray

Cover design by – Mr.Ash

Book formatting- Ishani Agarwal

ISBN: 978-93-89557-24-4

Open Genre

1st Edition

<u>DISCLAIMER</u>

This is a work of fiction. Our editors have tried their best to edit the content of all the author/authors and check the plagiarism.

All the write-ups in this book are unique and are only published in this book.

In case any plagiarism or error is found, only the author is responsible alone, and not the publisher.

ACKNOWLEDGEMENT :

The success and final outcome of this project required a lot of guidance and assistance from many people and I am extremely privileged to have got this all along the completion of my project. All that I have done is only due to such supervision and assistance and I would not forget to thank them. I respect and thank Mr. Ashutosh Das and Ms Rubal Choudhury for providing me an opportunity to do the project work in BookSquirrel Publication House and giving me and all support and guidance which made me complete the project duly. I am extremely thankful to him for providing such a nice support and guidance, although he had busy schedule managing the corporate affairs. I owe my deep gratitude to my project guide to my grandfather who always took keen interest on my work and guided me all along, till the completion of my work by encouraging me the right path of my life by providing all the necessary information for developing myself .I would not forget to my parent's contribution since birth to till now for their encouragement and more over for their timely support and guidance till the completion of our project work .I am thankful to and fortunate enough to get constant encouragement, support and guidance from all my friends which helped me in successfully completing my project work. Also, I would like to extend my gratefulness to my people who everyday inspires me to think about the society in a different way special way and specially Ashtami didi and her family. Lastly I would like to thank all the writers who have worked hard and have made an effort for this book to be successful.

TWISHA RAY

Instagram Id : the_scripturient_girl.

" Co-author for Ink Drift Hug stories ","Ink Drift Fear Stories", " Empower Women Empower Society", and "Colors of Dreams".

She is a hardworker. She have seen so many ups and downs in her life. Though she always stand back and overcame these obstacles. So she never giving up attitude makes her strong. She is a good motivator and she also have good communication and interpretational skills is a computer science engineer and a writer , writes about society , poems story writer and blogger from the city of joy Kolkata west Bengal. She has been writing since the age of

4 and she got her poetry featured in newspapers and online portals. Fond of music , learning new

languages traveling photography and literature, she manages to take her readers to a charismatic world of inspiration of her life.

She has been writing many quotes, published and featured poems, many stories and she is ' Literature Captain ' on StoryMirror app. She has been a moderator in Yoalfaaz and other places . Co-author in 8 anthologies and worked as compiler under 1 publication house compiler . She is a person of value and deep affection. In her nature and writing, you will find a peace and her aim is to inspire everyone in the world and she is in your quotes

A moment

Take a moment.
Put the alarming behind.
Grab in the beauty around.
Let it unwind your mind.
Watch the golden glow
Of the rising morning sun.
Embrace the peaceful aura
Of the break of dawn.
Savor the soft caress
Of the gently moving breeze.
Listen to its nifty tune
Among the swaying trees.
Enjoy the lovely scene
Of a floating butterfly.
Graceful flight and happy tweets
Of a bird perched up high.

Peruse the evening sky
In its outstanding splendor.
The wide and open pallet
Merging shapes and colors.
Relish the loving sight
Of children having fun,
Skipping feet and carefree voices
Under the setting sun.
Spare a still moment
Every once in a while.
Take in the beauty around.
Take it in with a smile.

<u>Inner Peace</u>

The wind whistles past my ears.
Plugging my eyes, I lose all my fears.
The waves strikes into the rocks.
Out here there is no time on my clock.

The peace I feel here just soothes my mind.
A peaceful day so hard to find.
The breeze just calms my soul.
Helps me think about what is my life's goal.

I then look out over the ocean,
And it feels like my life has lost its commotion.
The sun sets down over the clouds.
But the orange glow around makes me proud.

As the night draws near.
I feel like where I need to be is here.
The soothing nature this afternoon brings
Just feels like such a beautiful thing.

I sit and wonder where life will go,
But right now all I want is for time to slow.
To enjoy this moment and feel free,
To clear my mind and find some glee.

It's days like these I truly treasure.
Amazing nights and beautiful weather.
It may not seem like much.
But it's moments like these I want to clutch.

For once I feel like life is bliss.

So many hard days in which my happiness was missed.
I could get lost listening to the waves.
Listening to the birds and watching how the clouds behave.

I could close my eyes and fade into the night.
The tranquility I feel helps me win the fight.
As the waves keep crashing into the rocks,
I feel the happiness in my heart become unlocked.

The day is drawing to a close.
The peacefulness I feel right now I'll only know.
Right now my mind is finally clear.
It's time to go as the night draws near.

Ahmar Siddiqui

Ahmar is a corporate slave and a hermit in the making. A sapiophilic and textrovert. Passionate about movies and music. Newbie at writing.

Wife/ Beloved As she was being wheeled towards the operation theater, he reached out and held her hand, walking along the stretcher. She held his hand tightly and a slight smile appeared on her lips. A tear dropped from her eye. He wiped it with his palm. As the doors of the OT opened to take her in, he leaned forward and whispered in her ear "I am waiting …" with moist eyes. Standing outside the OT door, in an alien city, all alone, at a very young age, on a cold wintry day, the four hours felt like eternity. As the door of the OT opened and she was ushered out on a stretcher encased in wires and tubes, he rushed towards her. Her eyes, still under the influence of anesthesia, were desperately searching for him. As their eyes met, they smiled faintly. No words were spoken. Don't have to. Her eyes were clearly saying "I came back for you". A wife had gone in and a beloved came out.

Anurag Mishra

INSTAGRAM ID : @myquoyes.04

Anurag Mishra From Mumbai Maharashtra.

कभी-कभी कुछ लोग,

माना किसी बात को, जाहिर नहीं करते।

लेकिन वो आप की परवाह बहुत करते है।

वो कोई और नहीं, हमारे माता पिता ही होते है ।

अगर किसी को वास्ताव में,

आप की फिक्र है।

तो वो आप के बिना बोले ही,

आप की हर बातों को समझ जाएगा ।

Aa Jaye maut magar,

Dil na Aaye Kishi par khuda, Tu Bula Le Apne pass par, Mohabbat na Kara ae Khuda.

स बदलती हुई दुनिया में, रोज नए चेहरे उबरते है।

कुछ रेह जाते पीछे, तो कुछ आगे को बड़ते है।

मेहनत जो करते है, उन्हीं को फल मिलते है।

इस बदलती हुई दुनिया में, रोज नए चेहरे उबरते है

Anjali

Insta Id : Thought_pen_5516

Here raining at that time all were running to make them safe from wet and too from the rain. I am also one among them i too don't like that much fresh sand smell and all the trees are enjoying the rain. Rain drop kisses the leaves. Flowers hugs the rain drops by seeing the nature the my mind is at peace and equanimity and so on..

My uncle was at next block he called me to have an evening snacks.. yaa it was already time it was late too here the thing lies baby while I was crossing I really don't know how you came there each and every rain drops shows u baby I was shocked and standing at that place middle of the way all are shouting as kunal come on....!!!!

I really lost my mind I started enjoying rain yes may be the reason was you at that time .I was chasing all the rain drops because your in that .It may be so crazy but I was good and you were so awesome in that too by that time rain suddenly stopped oh my gosh no rain so no face .Then I remembered my uncle called me I went I got my snacks and I started to enjoying my snacks there is a question strikes in my mind how you came there at that time my mom shouted wake up Kunal its   6AM . After wake up I realized that it was a dream. Though, it was a dream I thought might be one day it would become into true in my life. My journey of life is flowing on and in search of that a cute angle.

He was in shadows and corridors of the wall which is sorrow and dark...he reflects my love which had flown away remembering the beats of the heart..you are the light that shines my darkest nights lights the dark corners of my heart with your love troubled some water in my souls calm down..

Balvendra Singh Chauhan

Balvendra Singh Chauhan is currently pursuing the long and never-ending stream of literature. He being a voracious reader tries to expand his domain to unlock new vistas of unexplored world. He hails from the serene land of Nainital that is well acknowledged across the globe for its beauty of nature. He also has deep interest in political talks and discussions. Apart from that, he is lover of music, cricket and distinct cuisines.

Brain is exhausted of rationalizing people, Completely bewildered in state of stifle. What heart feels, mind completely denies, Exposed facade of people is merely suffice. Acquaint of mine suggested me critical thinking, To broaden horizon, uplifting from surficial blinking. It vividly displayed that world isn't real, Else is series of pseudo melodramatic serial. Faith of one is crumpled as paper, Thrown in garbage as useless wrapper. Sensitivity isn't confined within girls' periphery, Rather holds space as well in boys' territory. Implemented the suggestion and practiced criticality, But resulted in nullifying this futile ability. More I intake, more I feel dejected, More I interact, more sensed infected. What's the cause of dejection, am I the one? Or just care and affection creating problem to someone. Or else expecting realistically is causing dejection, Or unbiological sibling's bond is creating objection. My love for loved ones is from heart, But this dejection is making me fall apart. Lord may help to contemplate my sadness, In order to shrink ever increasing critical vividness.

Universe is completely materialistic in nature, Whenever require most, it abandons creature. Leaves it alone at its condition, Dying or living, on its own apprehension. Rigidity is such enjoys one's failure, Displays subversion of nature, as they are cavalier. Hypocrisy, biasedness, double entendreness is ruling Such traits in society are growing and schooling. Trust, faith, loyalty deviated from pathway, Hate, jealousy, fallacy substituted its Ray. Circle of hope, shrinked with time's lapse, Confined within boundary, of own beneficiary steps. No matter how better one expresses feeling, But faces critical analysis, instead of healing. Eulogized rendering converts kind person to adamant, Who learn norms, in midst of society's being malevolent. Post-modernism excelled advancement with scepticism, Reframed emotions in form of symbolism. Socialization changed abruptly, forgotten third gen, In lieu lead to, fall in values and inspiration.

Mechanisation turned kids into technical setup, Once get stuck, feels depressingly fedup. Balancing science with culture, will lead society's restore, Serving humanity over individuality, advances ailment cure.

Violent gushes of innate psychic, Hobbles implicitly whole physic. Disbalances the social equilibrium, Muddles over acquainted mapparium. Heated brain multiplies reaction, And nullifies responsive action. Universe proclaim it's anchor, Body's devil named as Anger. Outbursts as volcanic eruption, Causes positive environmental deduction. Molten lava dwindles head, Swivelled notion widely spread. Turns attitude as fiery, Moulds person as dreary. Elongates ruckus of negativity, Dislodges bails of sublimity. Anger's act is midnight black, Hollow surface with hollow stack. Null gravity with void sustainity, This is anger's sole identity. No matter how fast grows, And how fast hit burrows . At the end calmness wins, Oversheds anger to the bins.

My world is woven around family, Whose members are connected sensually. Each one is my food and breath, And they are my ultimate strength. Illusion may come and may grow, But can't hinder trust that flow. Remains intact, undisturbed by outsourced unethics, Such is magic of family Dynamics Certain members are of certain forms, Some are genius and some book worms. Pleasure is mine that I am one, Who's not similar like anyone. Happiness comes within through poetry, Creating something to reveal life's mystery. It's way to know more about them, After life it becomes requiem. Life trespasses sometimes with those, Requires belonging in my life of whose. They become part of my primary group, Invictus sailor of acquainted troop. Designation to them is already assigned, wishful role is as well defined. Mere YES from theirs is left remember, To turn friend into family member.

My life seems as retreating wave, For whose arrival island crave. Such is condition of mine now, Waiting for splash to sprinkle anyhow. Each passing day is like year, Wanting to bring my dear near. Mere glance brings absolute Harmony, Aligns the crushed soul in disharmony. Separation bulges true nature within, Without that being can't live in. Survival issue comes along way, Proving others as fickle and fey. My might is mightier than other, Height of Love's like dove's feather. To express feelings is in mind, Waiting for right time to grind. Life which is simple and smooth, Was once perplexed and uncouth. Glorious dazzle has changed at once, All those polarizing factors renunce. Acts as anchor in my life, Opens sacred path and ends strife. It's that power of my soul, Which makes us one and does roll.

Bhavnit Katesarin Singhsachakul

Instagram ID: thewomanmatters

Bhavnit Katesarin Singhsachakul is the Executive Director of Qonsultant Pte. Ltd. She is also the Co-Author and Book Strategist of international bestseller 'The Equilibrium: Training the Money Mindset.' Apart from exploring her flair for words, her hobbies include adventure sports and cardio workouts. Bhavnit Katesarin is married to Businessman Sutheep Singhsachakul and they have one son Keshav Singhsachakul.

When the Queen rises to face the storm's wrath,

She becomes the eye of it.

We are all human;

But are we all engaging in Humanity?

Raise your inner stability so high

That the world becomes afraid to conquer you.

To be ahead of time,

Find the oasis before,

Before the throat gets parched.

When I've asked for the rains,

I walk out with an umbrella.

Debtanu Banerjee

Call it a twist of destiny, but a fan or fine arts and literature found shelter in the abode medicine. Wanting to illuminate the world with the fury of my quill,life gifted me with gold medals which I seemed to win at will. Doctor by profession, teacher by choice,writer by passion,musician...to rejoice....Last but not the least,a human being you can count on if you are not happy with your life. Yes I can't gift you with immortality or eternal mirth but atleast you'll no longer regret your birth.

Instagram Id : debtanubanerjee

WRITE UP 1

Once upon a time I tried to be somebody's everything... I lost friends and Tried to become somebody's something. There came a time, depression whispered You are nobody's something... Maturity arrived when I started trying To become everybody's something... But deep within I still smile As I realize that I am nobody's anything...

WRITE UP 2

As you grow old Everything you knew Seems to be a myth You gain wisdom You lose friends Your circle becomes bigger And your near ones, lesser At times you just yearn For a small cottage By a riverside To rest in the breeze With some good company Yet, in the mirage of False smiles, useless riches, Hidden tears and silent goodbyes Somewhere. Time flies...

WRITE UP 3

Silence speaks a thousand words... If your eyes can hear the noise, Close your eyes and you shall hear The throbbing heart's silent voice... Whether you listen, or ignore... Is your choice , I say for sure... But once the beats do stop, my dear You shall no longer find a cure... Learn to read between the lines, A wound within shall drip and bleed. Unless you find a cure to it, Depression and gloom, it shall breed. A smile does not mean they're coy, A human heart is not a toy, A soothing touch, it'll surely need.

WRITE UP 4

"There is no bitter phase than truth There is no better face than truth Its better to smile and die... Than to live with a burden and cry..."

Devika Radhakrishnan

INSTAGRAM ID : devika_1303

Avid reader. Obsessed with books. My inspiration to write is my life. My situations provoke me to write. Its makes me to know more of myself.

<u>DESIDERIUM</u>

I feel impotent,

My dreams are shattered,

Dreams!

I painted my childhood days,

Anticipated to have accomplished,

Turned to be a fiasco now.

Consenting my fate and moving on,

With a heavy heart,

Pushing each second in fathomless distress,

Why me? Only me!

Where I feel like an artist,

Whose painting water spilt,

Wrecked and desolated!!

<u>ENIGMA</u>

Somewhere profoundly I,

Ascertain a hunch of vacuity,

Unable to apprehend, the reason causing.

Exasperating every now and then,

Clutched on to me like,

There's no plan to leave.

Constantly probing,

Unable to resolve.

Where am I wrong?

Fabricating hiatus everywhere!

Where I'm impotent to do anything.

<u>AVOIR ENVIE</u>

A happy world where

I wish to be,

Where smiling faces wishing me,

No face as long as fiddle around,

This is all I want to see.

A desire to flutter in the welkin,

Every nook and corner to visit,

Searching the happy me!

Unable to reach this world still!

The evil thread so binding me,

Let me go -o- let me go.

Losing the breath, worth every now.

I am damn.

Dragged back to the same dark world!

Deep De

Deep De , he is a student of English literature , a poet , a movie reviewer and an heritage activist from the city of lights, Chandernagore , West Bengal.

Tragic Truisms by , Deep De Brave and valorous were his deeds , Fortune's favourite child was he ; Who stood against an era of darkness , And filled everywhere with a joyous glee . He tempted all with the bliss of freedom ; And acted as the igniter of hope ; But no one expected his tyrannous reign , As it was covered with liberty's robe . Not able to strike the golden mean , He became a subject of scorn for all . The greatest powers joined hands to conduct , One of history's most tragic fall . But if he pursued the middle path , Could he be , the great Napoleon Bonaparte ?

<u>Love's Sonetto</u>

The bird yearns for the greatest heights , A moth for the light , Humans crave for something dazzling , Though they are always encompassed by love's bright . For it is shallowness of human nature , By which enticed by glossy masking ; They very often neglect the real riches , And disdain the pleasant warmth of love's basking . But true feelings of endearment are so sincere , That it withstands all impediments . Lovers find solace , and rise above fear ; And the passions never din with dime sentiments . Truest Love always triumphs over haughty hate , And the sweet moments of bliss outlive the tortures of fate .

Dhaval Dilip Sangtani

Instagram Id :- @an__anonymous__writer

He is pursuing bachelor's of commerce, third year, and writing is his hobby. He thinks that penning down his deepest thoughts motivates himself, and if possible than he would make career out of his hobby. Apart from that, he loves to explore new things that bring along knowledge with them.

No one was there to encourage me the way i was left lonely behind my deadly thoughts the way i broke down i wont thought to be back onto the track the harshness was broken the calmness was all stolen the hope that i lost already by leaving with the fake dialogue were being my encouragement that's were though fake which were shown by me for their sake hopes were somewhere unexpected to come back but somewhere from long far away its proved me wrong once again the way you support me i can't express it into the few lines if i am here because you holding you from the past to the present and all over the future i assure you to live in my present for the better future the energetic spirit you have given me brought me back once again on a right track positiveness or negativeness its just a part of a game but the support love and to hold on in present for the future is what taught indirectly from their although the distance is their between two of us but i assure you to be with you not only holding your hand but holding your heart ill work hard to chase the hopes which you wanted to have missing isn't a solution all the time i know but it's hurt in the present but living with the memories which we had the past have been spent to live upon you to live to chase the dreams which you have that's the aim i assure i request you today wherever you are listen this please for my sake i promise you to chase to fullfil all the things that you shared.... :-Dhaval Dilip Sangtani

Juweriya Waseem

Insta id : Weizhi__girl

If we are influencers then we are also noxious , If we can create then we can destroy too but to be true We just want to influence you in a good way .. A dreamer , who .is writing out her heart in her teen days.

An Artist is someone who showers his love for the words by his Experiences and experiments ..

We seems to be brave and Skilled but from inside we are also like a blooming bud that fears to be plucked in between .

There are some incomplete but very deep phrases, That accommodate the sphere of our thoughts . One such phrase in this universe is life , Which is full of sentences but still an incomplete phrase , That is full of meaning but too deep to be discovered whole , Many tried to make it meaningful but none can make it complete . The silence of life is a loud echo , And the world was dumb but some of them were able to listen to it's pace . Everyone is trying to complete the phrase , and also to find the lost pieces , But little did they knew that they are only some few words of the incomplete phrase . Some went to change the scenario so far , But ended up only some miles apart . And in between the whole walk , They got to know about the diversity of the phrase . And also discovered , It will end up nowhere , As we are only few words in that race , And also the distance is too large to be traced . And as said before there are some deep but incomplete phrase.

Stars in the daylight - Our universe is a place that is full of stars and light , And also on our earth we have such stars in our sky , But these stars shines only in the moonlight !! Then what about the rest of the day , In the day light the stars that flatter on the ground are also able to compete those stars in the sky . Some shines with a mike or sometimes with a pen or may be with some paints and threads ! They shine on the ground but their sparkle covers all the sky !! And that's why they are called stars in the daylight.

The last note - After completing all her work she looked at the old wooden clock and smiled with happiness in her eyes , That she was done with her work and now she can go for a long drive with him !! She checked her phone , But no new notification pinged her up . She murmured May be he wanted to give her surprise , And started to dress up in one of her beautiful skirts !! And then combed her hair and applied some Shimmers and perfume as well . She stepped out the door and to meet him in the garden But as she tried to took her bicycle , she found a letter in her basket in which it was written " That we are no more together and yes I want my freedom back but surely we will be friends for the rest of life " . After reading the letter she got shattered in pieces and .

Mohnish

Insta id :moh_nish_99

I live in reality, but my dreams are yet to be true. Born as forever a student. Dissolved in pain, but still can fake a smile. Flunked to smile but a pro to lie. I play numb, but i ain't a dumb.

I'm a liar and am not worried about it. I'm only upset about the truth behind, being called a cheat. I'm a soul and now i regret to breath. All the scars on my ribs and the half broken wall changed me to an EXTROVERT.

I was born nothing with, dead emotions and no pain. But raised with veins puffing pain and face faking emotions.

From the time I was nine till the calendar turned 2k19, sadness never left my door knocked.

I still remember, I was nine when i last kissed happiness. Since then i been dreaming, eyes opened.

<u>Secrets aren't always dark bad!</u>

It is believed that i been walking bad, but i know the real reason i carried you down from past.
it was asked a million time to spread it open and not close, but i know how heavy that it can tear hearts apart.
i don't care if i'm counted good or bad in the minds of my blood,i know myself.

<u>Memories are sometimes painful!</u>

It is a bless for the people with mental health,
but it's a pain for the one's with the past mental issues.
it neither helped me grow nor left me happy,
but it gifted me blindness in the name of being a broad minded.
it left my wounds open for the words to slash my nerves again and again,
but it made me feel immortal that ground resists to sing.

<u>Regret ruined my past, present and future.</u>

It is all i carried from the past blue and red.
it is all i remember since the past alone and bleeding.
it is all i had to breathe to hold my heart under chest.
it's all i would never ever like to see you carrying, it's mine only mine.

Mohini Malipeddi

Insta Id :

Mohini, a house maker, writes about love and life. Passionate about writing and singing songs. A nature lover and a truth seeker at heart. Loves to learn and learns to love through her words.

In faith I'm the roots In persistence, the stem In hope I'm the bud In bliss, I'm the flower In love, I'm the shade In patience, I'm a TREE I'll wait for you forever Even if you have no heart for me!

Some unknown unseen unbound missing strands are making their way towards me . Am I going to discover a different world or the world is going to discover or a whole new different version of me.

From the ocean of love That resides in my eyes Drop the pearls of my dreams scattered are shores . How long, would they hold? Listen! Every pearl is narrating the tales that remained untold every word flowing from my heart every word dedicated to you.

For some its a bliss, for some its a pain For some its a loss, for some its a gain For some its a dream, for some its a truth For some its a life, for some its a death But in every form, love is an inevitable concept!

Neha kaira

Insta Id : Yard_of_thoughts

<u>Flower stuck in a vase.</u>

His disloyalty defines me atleast this is what society see. as I'm here to act like his teacher to turn him a human from a weird creature. his morals and values should become high he should forget how to lie. and if he fails to become a gentleman in the one responsible as this is not what i can. his disloyalty defines me.

We are not us anymore. when was the last time you hold my hand while driving ? you think I'm living but I'm just surviving. when was the last time we had a deep conversation ? more about our love, not life, career and education. when was the last time you asked me if I'm okay ? bought me books, chocolates and bouquet. when was the last time you said to me i love you ? it's been long, do you still ? i have no clue. we are not us anymore

I won't burn another fire, would kill all the love desire. I won't let these lips kiss another one, will give up these flings and fun. i won't see in another one's eyes, will prefer being blind while seeing other guys. i won't fall in love all over again, as you are and always will be my main.

May be the world has always seen the brighter side of yours. but i have seen your disease and the medicine that cures. In a room full of people where you fake your interest and smokes. i be the one at home with whom you share your lame jokes. With your so called friends, whenever you're out for drinking. Always come back to me, with your eyes blinking. and by all this, I'm not here to prove that I'm the one for you or you are the one for me. But if you are the last flower in this world, then I'm the only queen bee.

I have seen so many parts of you. some are good, but some bad too. sometimes you are the sky that is blue. or a memory loss person who has no clue. sometimes like a flower spreading it's glory or a psychic patient telling his story. sometimes like an umbrella who saves people from rain. but sometimes like a killer who like seeing people in pain. but I'm not here to love only good parts of you. as if you are a killer, I am a lover too.

Pranshi Agrawal

Insta id : agrawal.pranshi812

A doctor trying to pen much more then prescriptions.. because words heal more then medicines can.

A letter saved in my drafts? Dear dad, I am sorry dad, sorry for learning his favourite dish not yours, Even when i knew its you who is waiting for years to taste my food I am sorry dad,sorry for reminding him to take his medicines, not you Even when i knew you tend to forget to yake them everytime.. I am sorry dad, sorry for talking him hours on videocall, not to you Evn when i knew you wait d whole week for my videocall.. I am sorry dad, sorry for moving mountains to make his day special and not yours Even when i knew its you who have planned all my surprises since childhood I am sorry dad, sorry for calling him first after my result Even when i knew its you who will be happiest I am sorry dad, sorry for lieing u evertym i am out with him and not you Even when i knew its you who save your every leave day for planning my vaccations I am sorry dad, sorry for saying him sorry and not you Even when i knew all u want just a lilttle realization on my part I am sorry dad, sorry for giving him all my attention not you Even when i knew a single call from me makes you happy I am sorry dad, sorry for allowing him to break ur princess heart..for making him my hero Even after knwoing that only you are superhero I am sorry dad, sorry for not having courage to send this letter to you..

So is your novel completed? Its almost done !! M working on last chapter - she said Its been more then 8months ,

 N u r still on last chapter - asked d publisher Yeah!! M waiting for him to come so that i can give happy ending to my love story - she said

Prerna Chhetri

Insta Id : Chhetriprerna000

My qualification is Master's degree in literature, I'm a hairstylist who have a passion for writing. Currently addicted to micro tales, Haikus and one-liners. "Just getting started" these words always keep me going.

I Got My Self Rescued. When you try to save yourself from fake spoof, all you end up is being used up by your own procrastination. Secondly, there are people who attack your anxiety dilemma, but you're already broken into pieces just like a shredded paper, even the tape would feel miserable and so the people's voices are like symphony doesn't have any regression. Then you read books about motivation, read quotes of success, when failure never trusted your path. Still the delusional list keeps moving up. You then open up for the public display of laughter and sympathy, declare you the product of Sadness. Where sadness is just a baby, the real deal is the Depression, no one knows. Then you walk down the lane of melancholy of Death, chocking down own soul in persuasion. For a last time you tried to open up. This time it's not him/her or those additional relatives but a psychiatrist. In response he/she will lead you a way to create a bit of future. Finally, you start noticing others of same kind. Broken soul in abandoned body. A relief I felt when I saw pain can be of many kind. So I took a hold of that hand and pull back up from that elderly bridge and save a life with a smile. Then she smiled back with a little hope on her eyes. So I hold her tight till her pain washed. Back home I remember my divine hand , mother as you say praying for my well being daily, not to mention I feel the part played by my pets. And your precious life is more precious now more than ever. Even though your anxiety sometimes screw things up, still you're working on it for self and for working on that same path as mine holding hands saving lives.

Title- Femme Tale. She was born to fight, Like her father in a Khakee, In the border of arms, With blood shed daily. She was a youngest of all, But a heart to fight a dragon, With that brightest smile, Tears don't have a chance. She was killed many time, But she leaned back against odds, With a mother so strong protecting, Giving hope of returning back. She was put to a test of loyalty, Let a thousand Agni Pariksha. Couldn't crumble her into ashes, Rose like a brave Phonenix. She is the voice of many, Together winning many battles, Together breaking stereo types, Together for the equality.

Rajendra Kurulkar

Insta id : Jheel_poet

Jheel "I am Rajendra Kurulkar an established fine artist and presently I am faculty at art and design department Sophia Polytechnic at Mumbai. Mentoring the art students since last 22years. Teaching as well as writing poetry is my passion. Both the journeys painting and writing poetry gives me immense pleasure I use both the space to explore my inner feelings. According to every word expressed has its own colour, tone, texture, hue and intensity. Both of them are my soul. I published all my poetry with my pen name "Jheel ".

जिंदगी यह जिंदगी अब तो आजमाना छोड़ दे, आँसू ओं मुस्सलसल् दिल से लगाना छोड़ दे! अपने अपने कह के ज़हर झील में मिला दिया, आँधीयों करों क़रम के वादीयाँ जलाना छोड़ दे! है मोहब्बत मुझको वतन के लोगों से कह दे, मेरे दोस्तों को ही अब दुश्मन बनाना छोड़ दे! शान है और इमान है दुनिया में हिन्दुस्तान मेरा, मज़हब के नाम पर बच्चों को डराना छोड़ दे! हाथों में नादान बच्चों के देते हैं हथियार क्यों, कच्चे ख्वाबों की आँखों में जन्नत सजाना छोड़ दे! कहीं ऐसा न लगें की जीने की तमन्ना ना रहें, अन्जाना कह कर मेरी लाश को जमाना छोड़ दे! जो बीत गया सो बीत चुका नई सुबह आने दे, इन्सान हो तुम इन्सान बनो ख़ुदा बनना छोड़ दे!

हमनें देखीं वह निगाहें खोई खोई क्यूँ न जाने, तसवीर दिल के आईने में सजाई क्यूँ न जाने! बाद यह मुद्दतें मिला कोई ऐसा जख़्म मुझको, बिन पूछे ही मिला हैं ऐसा सौदाई क्यूँ न जाने! हमनें माँगी थी दुवाएँ रात दिन जिनके ख़ातिर, मिलने के पहले मिली यह जुदाई क्यूँ न जाने! हमनें उनकों यह कहा नहीं ऐतबार कर लेना, दर्द से इश्क़ की चिंगारी ए जलाई क्यूँ न जाने! भूल करते रहें हम उनसे मोहब्बत करने की, जाने किस में है किस की भलाई क्यूँ न जाने! कब जमाना था अच्छा कोई मुझको बताओं, सब की आद्त हैं सब की बुराई क्यूँ न जाने! वह समझदार है बहोत यह ख़ुदा ने कह दिया, झील की यह इबाद्त है हरजाई क्यूँ न जाने! दोस्त बन बन कर निकले दोस्तों लूटने वाले, किस किस को दे हम यह सफ़ाई क्यूँ न जाने!

हरे पत्तों का रंग वक़्त के साथ साथ बदलते हुए देखा है, हमनें भी हर ख्वाब ए ख़यालों को बिख़रते हुए देखा है! जितने भी आये जमाने कुछ

कर दिखाने की उम्मीद से, किया बहोत शराफ़त से उनकों भी गुज़रते हुए देखा है! चाँद और सूरज ने मोहब्बत को मिल बाँट के जिंदा रखा, हर सुबह और हर शाम को फ़िर भी सुलग़ते हुए देखा है! यह जिंदगी तो एक सहरा हैं धूप में निकलती रहती है, फ़िर भी एक ख़ामोश आईने को मुस्कुराते हुए देखा है! जिंदगी की ख़ोज में निकला हमसफ़र वहीं का रह गया, एक बुढी माँ के आँचल को भी हमनें तरसते हुए देखा है! पानी पानी कहतें कहतें हर गाँव कहाँ से कहाँ तक गया, बेवज़ह बरसात से इन किसानों को मरते हुए देखा है! आँसू छुपा कर हँसते हँसते जीने की आदत हैं झील को, हर सुबह छाँव को सूरज की तरह सरक़ते हुए देखा है!

देखूँ तुझको ही मैं अगर न देखूँ तो हमसफ़र ही क्या, तेरी ख़ुशबू से अगर सांस ही न चलें तो हश्र ही क्या! तिर ए दिल पे मेरे क्या चलाया हैं तुने ऐ हमनबी मेरे, ज़हर ही अगर जिंदा रख दे मुझको तो असर ही क्या! तेरी मौजूदगी हैं ख़ामोशीयों में जो रात रोशन कर दे, हर एक शेर न लिख दो चिराग़ो में तो बसर ही क्या! क़तरा क़तरा ख़ुन से अगर अलग अलग कर दे कोई, नाम इश्तेहार ए मोहब्बत पे न छपा तो ख़बर ही क्या! मैं चला जाता हूँ जब भी जहाँ भी तेरा साँया होता हैं, जो न रखें ख़याल ए दीवाने का तो वह नज़र ही क्या! तुम चले आये अगर सारी दुनिया ही छोड़ कर कभी, तु मुस्कुरा दे और बहार ही न खिलें तो शज़र ही क्या! उम्र ए कैद मेरी तब जाकर हुई हैं ऐ हँसीन ए क़ातिल, क़सर है कोई नाम न आये तो झील की क़ब्र ही क्या!

Rahul Maurya

Insta id : @the__creative__pen__

I'm a graduation student. And as per my hobbies I use to write some poetries, quotes and life related stories. I write by my own experiences or society observations.

STORY OF 12th PASSOUT STUDENTS "18" ye age hi aise hoti hai sayad....ki bache bade ho jate hai, Jimmedariyon ko samjhane lagate hai, Bhavishya ki chinta karne lag jate hai. Aksar ye har 12th pass karne wale students ke sath hota hai wo iss mode par aa kar ek bar confuse ho hi jate hai ki kon sa rasta chunana hai. Aakhir ho bhi kyu na life me first time kuchh chunane ja rahe hote hai. Ye jindgi ka aisa chauraha hai jaha har koi aa kar ek bar sochta jarur hai ki kon sa rasta chunu. Khair manjil sabki ek hi hoti hai.... paise kamana, bas raste alag alag hote hai. Gole to hum bahut pehle hi tay kar liye hote hai bas raste nahi pata hote hai. Aise mod par hum kisi senior ke salah ke kafi jarurat mand hote hai. Iss chaurahe par agar koi achha marg darshak mil jaye to raste aasan ho jaye. Aise me hume unn logo ki jarurat hoti hai jo ki hume bata sake ki humare gole ko achieve karne ke liye kon sa rasta jyada sahi hoga. Chuki internet par sab available hai fir bhi jo humari jigyasa hoti hai wo internet se nahi mit pati. Aise me kabhi kisi ka year bhi gap ho jata hai, jo ki mere manne se bahut badi galti hoti hai. Kyuki usse padhai me continuity nahi rah pati. Aur kafi problems aati hai dubara padhai shuru karne me. Aur aise me humare surroundings ka bhi kafi asar padta hai. Agar koi classmate kahi apni padhai shuru kar deta hai to log compare karna shuru kar dete hai, jo ki bahut galt hai. Jiske wajah se hum depression me jate hai aur jaldbaji me galt rasta chun lete hai. Actually uss time hume khud ko janana hota hai, khud ki capability, strength ki janch karni hoti hai. Koi dusra kya kar raha hai usse fark nahi padna chahiye. Sabki capability (aukat) alag alag hoti hai. Apane strength ko apna hathiyar banana chahiye.

Riddhi Karia

Instaid : riddhi_karia

They say that reading and writing is my escape from reality, But little do they know for me it is what prism is to white beam of light.

"This too shall pass, It's just a phase, Cheer up, lighten up, Sing along the winds, And groove to the beats," They told me. Is it that shameful dad, to be deceived by the depths of depression? "Don't think about it", you say "The more you think, the more you feel". Feel! What do I feel? "Drowning" Dawn to dusk drowning in the darkness, but never hitting the rock bottom. Wondering what it's like to face death? Or shall I say, "Numb". Numb with dead dreams in the corner of my eyes, Flames of burning hope in the heart like a lantern aloof in the midst of a stormy sea, Gasping, gasping, In the emptiness Barely breathing, Will I ever come back to the shore again, No starving sky to guide my way. Bridges break and bridges burn, How does it feel to be abandoned by one's soul? The say that sun shines the brightest after the most darkest hour, Will I survive to see the sun shine again? What shall be done when in war with your own self? Who shall win? Who shall loose? At what price shall I choose? "This too shall pass, It's just a phase, Cheer up, lighten up, Sing along the winds, And groove to the beats," They told me.

Need to find my way back to myself, What shall be done when all that you have known turns against thyself? Burnt to the ground, As your world stops turning round, Dreams turned to ashes, You must free yourself from your own cages, For when you think the light is gone leaving you in the ocean of perplexity, Thou shall rise, After they fall, for the phonenix rises from the ashes, incredible to all.

Are day and night meant to be together? She wondered, As he was the social butterfly and she was the one lurking behind the shadows.

Slipping right down the slope, Dying desire to climb the mountain top. All that you have known about yourself has betrayed you, How do you plan to stay sane and start anew? When the darkness surrounding you starts dimming your own light, Hold on to yourself, be your own guide. When you feel the sea is sinking you, You are the only one you can count on for rescue. When your decorated dreams turn to pieces, Flickr of flames burning in the longing eyes ceases, Reignite those sparks, For history awaits time of your benchmark, Show those stormy tides, The tornado you hold inside never dies.

Rishabh Katiyar

Insta id : rishabhkatiyar_1611

Born to Express not to Impress. Writes everything what other are hesitate to write or express.

When everything goes wrong
and nothing seems ever right
i know i can always run back to you
in your arms i will ever be safe

there is so much stress all around
my boss screams at me all day long
the customers i serve all crib and whine
no one is ever satisfied

its a mad race to be on top
ace with pace , get medals and rewards
under so much stress i can never ever shine
i break under stress, i yearn to fast forward the time

i dream of you ever more
under your walls i feel safe
walking on your floor everything seems fine
the soft and sweet my comfy bed
always gives the chills, i am ever on cloud nine
can't wait for the clock to strike five
to pack my bag and leave this hell hole
to run to you , oh my SWEET HOME

<u>Dear Little One,</u>

This world might feel a little strange,
Your mother may be a bit deranged,
Society will "fix you" and arrange,
But your pure essence will never change.

This life is not garunteed,
It wants you to drip and bleed.
Your demons will claw and feed,
Construe your thoughts and mislead.

I know you want to write that letter,
But it's supposed to get way better.
Use those words as a comfy sweater,
But the devil knows your a debtor.

I know death seems quite inviting,
But I want you to keep on fighting.
Even though the temptations are biting,
Take this life and do some rewriting.

I wish I had all the answers for you,
Knew the future through and through,
Give you something to look forward too,
And tell you lies that are so untrue.

It might get better, it might get worse,
Life, in reality, is just a curse,
A rollercoaster and a hearse,
But take those reigns and reverse.

Saurav Banerjee

Insta id : unrevealedself

I'm from Aligarh, U.P. Currently I'm pursuing my graduation from arts stream. I also published my first poetry collection book "Words Of Heart" in the month of July, 2019 in amazon website if one want's to grab it search for it.

Chase your dreams No matter how difficult it seems You've to do one thing Don't care what others might think Just keep your aim clear and clean That shouldn't become deem Remember, your willpower is your team If you're getting what I mean.

There are many things to say, just need a listener.
There are many things to write, just need a reader.
There are many wounds in world, just need a healer.

The things you do happily and with all your attention on that particular thing, that thing will always be done perfectly and it'll bring a lot of satisfaction with understanding.

This world is a beautiful place.
Everyone and everything is beautiful in their own unique way. But somehow we're unable to see them as we are more focused on the things we don't want.

Sarika Attri

Insta id : Sarikasmic

I'm sarika . I love reading books . I'm also a dancer. I'm from himachal and a bcs graduate.

I was born and first heard a sound "You'll become a pilot and make us proud". My future was decided by my dad and mum Nobody asked me what I wanted to become Maybe my parents had seen wings in my brain They wanted to give me sky but I wanted paper and pen Finally I decided to tell truth to dad But I was frightened that he'll become sad After so much hustle I wrote a letter Gave it to dad and somewhere feeling better The thing I never explained in 20 years of my life That 20 lines letter had power with no strife And that day I again heard a sound "You'll become a writer and make us proud".

In our whole life we are always taught that "don't judge the book by the cover". But I have a question for you......if you think that book is so good from inside then why don't you try to improve the cover. It is very easy to live in the myth, but the real human is that who accept the truth. Whenever life gives you reasons to die, be brave,stand up and give life a high five. Try to get out of your comfort zone, do those things that are difficult to hold upon.

Samruddhi Kapgate

Insta id : @Wordwards

Happy and sad, sometimes sane and mostly mad, lifts wieght and kicks bad, just a simple, sexy and a crazy women.

Only if I had.. Those arms around me Only if I had.. Someone who is godly Only if I had.. The worth to make it through Only if I had.. Someone who loved me true Only if I had.. Someone's memories to pelv Only if I had.. A heart alive, now dead in the grave.

Weary eyes and long walks, Dramatic life with hopes off, How could it be a problem, That nobody bothers But the life is empty and the time's off Couldn't imaging what's right and wrong, Always heading with my gut strong, Broken and bizzare those terrible nightmares, How do I wake up with my smile on ?

The clouds and the thunders, Rain down to wonders, A flick away from those blunders, Reasons to forget sunders, For some a moment, For some a pain, For some a dancing platform, For some a rejoice to brain, When it comes it recalls memories, Childhood laughs and rainy savouries, Swaying trees and windy rains, That slight breeze fantastically comes again, When no one stays, It mends your ways, The sinking boat thenproudly sails.

Layer on layers, Hiding the darkness within, The bad inside you grinning. Layers on layers, You kept exfoliating, Trying and tiring to stop skinning.

Layers on layers, The real face reavlealed, Watching the reality you retreat. Layers on layers, Falling apart, Sheding the unreal, You realise it's just the start.

I asked God for happiness, He handed me a family, Said 'look after them'. I asked God for success, He gifted me intelligence, Said 'make good use of it'. I asked God for love, He sent an angel, Said 'never let it go'. I asked God for my answers, He showed me omens, Said 'discover your path'. And the moment I had all of it, God called me to him. Said 'lets start it all over'.

Samrudhi Patil

Insta id :The_ignited_mind15

Samrudhi Patil is from Pune, Maharashtra (India). She's currently pursuing Bachelor of Arts. Her interest in writing developed during her Junior College, during which she has written many articles, poems and write-ups. Writing for her, is an escape from the real world. Her articles are a mixture of her experiences, her emotions with a pinch of practicality. In life, her aim is to heal, to grow, to live.

Write up 1

I was a bud, Tiny and innocent. My petals were closed, My color, resplendent. I bloomed the next day, Was I bright and cheery. My cheeks were flushed Visible to all clearly. The other flowers Were red with rage Maybe they hated how I had everyone's gaze. When I was in my color They tried to pluck me. But soon after I wilted They did not even see. I realised then Life works this way - People being nice to you Till the end of the day. They wont care about you Or your feelings. They're going to be selfish As if it's a business dealing. But forget not, I still stand strong. Because not to others, But to me, I belong.

Write up 2

From leaving friends then after a fight, to leaving the WhatsApp group today, with time changed our social norms.

Write up 3

When I was a kid, he taught me to maintain a balance while riding a cycle. Today he teaches me to maintain a balance my family and my job. Father are, indeed, pillars of support no matter what stage of life it is.

Saswati Behera

Insta id : lisa.saswati

Currently i am pursuing my btech in biotechnology in CET,Bhubaneswar.I have completed my 12th in 2019. Writing is something which comes from within and i love doing that.

THE UNEXPECTED MEETING

Meeting you was neither a coincidence for me nor for you,
You have shared many things or I can say a part of you.

Felt connected to you ,the moment i met
Someone has truely said "its never too late"..

I was in hurt ,I was in pain
Holding my hand you loved me as much as you can.

Did lost all the hopes of gettng happy again
Bt you made all the ways out and showered me wid the love of
rain.

AFTER YOU LEFT

The day seem to be as dark as night today,
Afterall you left,breaking all the promises you made one day.

There's no answer to the question"how much i loved you?"
But ,would definitely say i did love you.

Wearing a smile definitely makes a girl beautiful,
No matter real or fake
When everything happening around you is horrible.

Yes, i did not stop you from going,
Because i knew making you stay will neither make you happy nor
me.

Its okay, if we are not holding each other's hand anymore,
All i needed was you to be happy more ...
and more.

Shraddha Padhi

Insta id : shradha.padhi

I believe stories can change the world. I write, therefore I am.Engineer by education, the moments I have experienced in my life have always inspired me to weave stories in my mind and help me write. Zoning into this one step at a time and enjoying the journey.

Write up 1

Love, The Vagrant Dweller A decade and more, summer winds just soar And of long long winters that still allure Of aspect more sublime, of those blessed times Of unremembered acts of kindness, blown away perchance My heart leaps anew from the deep deep slumber Thoughts of seclusion wander to the quiet of the sky Shed off the weary weight of the mighty repose Clad in thoughts of piety, dubiety wanders by Reflection of soul revives, eluding the fretful stir You gave me a forever within limited days of my being Recompensed for the wilts of daily life Grateful am to thee Be Inherent, matured and do stay Oh love the vagrant dweller, Have you heard what I had to say?

Write up 2

The Journey I have taken longer than I promised! I am almost there now! I feel I no longer guide the path Its completely on its own The love and light I speak of This is where dreams are born So many stories in the making little chapters each day Glorious Powerful connects so resplendent Puts fedoras on my greys Dabbled in some magic moments learning and exploring further Inspiration from mundane could be cliche But when its done right There's nothing any better.

Write up 3

Little Chapters On life's lanes Learnings so deep Tuned into the love and light And still in no hurry On the road of indigenous life. A journey of sustainability And the giggles in between A life of constant exploration Following nothing but the dreams. Set out on a new regime Self funded the culture we regard Not old not young I thrive Fabulously in the stories I guard. I bow in humility and listen As they matter more and more we all connect to the fables Rejuvenation galore. The heart sings the same song stay inspired,be the glow Be absorbed and be lost into the flow So driven by clarity, free of ego lets be the passionate doers Desperate to grow, Be wise, breathe and come keep lighting up homes.

Write up 4

Forebearers of My Life!! For the forebearer duo who gifted me with life Childhood and adolescence and all things upright My models of self-transcendence Beacons of wisdom for my dangling ignorance. The ever candid and patient answers to my strange questions Pillars of strength for my vanishing fears Showered me with selfless never ending love Made the moody, elegiac moments disappear with the only hope I love them back and "I will forever" could there be a sweeter agreement? I swear. The freedom explained and lived And that I hold onto still Sheltered from unknown and proverbial dangers Expounded to be fearless in facing them too. How seamlessly they blend moments of despair Abate their sadness by comfort and care Sometimes I wonder what common traits they share Their upbringing echoes through my heart I bare. They are always listening Wish I could hear what are they thinking Sharpened emotional outreach Active alert senses do preach Simple profound thoughts and what not. Beyond limitations Each unproven uproar they fought Different roads, But one destination they sought.

Write up 5

"Woman" I said... "who are you", he asked "Woman" I said rubbed off each one's lives sinked behind the slammed doors tattered thoughts and covered wounds strapped to traditional vales of mud Yet strong to roar in silence Spiked with humour and intelligence Bright and new each day like the early Sun rays Sneaking through the uncovered window bars Bitten inside, undaunted of those scars Wonder-eyed kid with rains in her eyes A picker of hopes dreams and broken hearts Empathetic, deeply humane and sensible Pleased with little, sacrificing galore Seldom applauded or revered Gleaming with Love more and more "Who are you" he asked again "Lass, bitch, damsel, wench" you see Woman is what I love to be.

Souvik Chatterjee

Insta id : Ninos_oeuvre

Myself Souvik Chatterjee... Currently studying Civil Engineering in Techno India Saltlake... Love to play with words and photography...

Write up 1

They said, "It's too easy to tear the ties of kinship and leave the world by killing yourself." One who just came back from the mouth of death replied, "It's far easier to live with all your problems than to kill yourself." He laughed and replied, "One dies to tear the ties of kinship, making it even stronger."

Write up 2

Before saying anything about anyone... Do keep yourself in their place first... Then say whatever you feel from there... Sometimes they too may be correct from their own place... Do think before you speak... As it's easy to break a bond... But it's hard to fix it again...

Write up 3

♥JOKER♥

 In this world everyone is like joker... Happy from outside, heart broken from inside... Don't believe me?? Look at yourself... Are you happy with your current belongings?? Are you happy with your current position?? Are you happy with your surroundings?? The answer will always be "NO!!!" YOU MIGHT BE HAPPY WITH THE ABOVE... But as soon as, Someone gets the post you think you deserve, Someone gets thing that you don't have, Someone went to the place you can't afford... EVERYONE HAS SOMETHING THEY WANT BUT CAN'T AFFORD... So everyone is just like joker... Happy from outside, heart broken from inside...

Write up 4

*** LOST ***

Somewhere in between everything and nothing... I lost my voice... Somewhere in between friends and foes... I lost my feelings... Somewhere in between success and failure... I lost my spirit... Somewhere in between accessible and isolated... I lost my vision... Somewhere in between peace and conflict... I lost my hearing... Somewhere in between love and hatred... I lost myself... Somewhere in between mine and myself... I lost everything...

Write up 5

♥ YOU - YOURSELF ♥

 You were always my partner in crimes... You were always my partner in mistakes... You were always my partner in everything... You were always there to help me... You were always there to support me... You were always there to love me... You were always there by my side... You were always there at my ups and downs... You were always there enjoying my happiness... You were always there crying on my sadness... You were always there when I needed someone... You were still there when I needed no-one... But... But I never noticed you... I never gave you the respect you deserve... I never gave you the love you deserve... I never gave you the time you deserve... But you still loved me... You still loved me while I was looking for love... While I disrespected you for someone else... While I wasted time on someone else... While I left you for someone else... Thank you for making me what I'm today... Thanks for always believing in me... And sorry for ignoring you...

Souvik khanra

Insta Id : Souvik26082000

I am Souvik khanra.. my Writing id is Dodon.. i am from singur, Hooghly.. i am a student of zoology hons.. under Calcutta university

Write up 1

Life is not a problem to be solved,, It is a reality to be experienced.. Life is not a bad dream.. It is a sunrise,, That reminds us of a new opportunity to live,, Never give up,, because ,, Life is just like a book,, In which everyday is a new page,, And.. Every page teach us a new value,,, Life is full of moments,, And every moments has a phase,, You have to analyse it's worth and timing,,

Write up 2

There is nothing wrong with me in my life,,, For not needing company,, I feel just fine.. When i am in my own.. Don't worry bout my health,, I can dance all by myself... Watch me be happy.. FOREVER ALONE

Write up 3

Life can be much better.. If you focus on the positive things.. No matter what hater says.. Your parents and who loves you truely,, Will stay in every situation... They help you and revive you in every situation.. So don't care about the negetive things.. Think positive,, hope positive,, One day, you will surely get success..

Sreeparna Ghosh

Insta id :

A foodie, travel freak, book lover, post-graduate in English. I am a firm believer of the fact that a pen is the most powerful weapon on earth. Thus, I took up writing as profession, absolutely by choice and not by chance.

Your success have many shareholders, your failures have none.

Ethics has been sabotaged brutally by immorality. Egomaniacal us has defeated all sensibility. For our sins we only have to pay, We are no wonder moving towards our doomsday. If you chose to bury your conscience in the darkness of greed, Sooner or later you only will be punished for your deed.

I don't seek comfort, In these race, Hankering after some avaricious quest. I don't seek comfort, In the world, Where humanity is dumped as waste. I seek comfort, In the solace that nature bestow, I long for a kiss of quietude anyhow.

A simple, straight forward NO, is always better than a meek, half hearted YES

..

Bring me the sunset in a cup, Let me savour it slowly, Let it titillate my senses, Let it's gusto enchant me wholly. But with the sunset, The mind is at war. While the twisted, cynical one, Provokes me to be forlorn. The cheery one says hold on, Because after every nightfall, Another pristine day is born.

Subhalaxmi Das

Insta Id : subha1428

A passionate writer, a singer, a motivational speaker, apart from these I am a Software engineer by profession. Love to fly high with eternal touch of nature. Challenging myself to be a part of every aspect of life.

I stop and stare ....Life is not all about happiness, enjoyment, motivation, move on. Sometimes life is all about the unseen chapters of a person, full of anxiety, sorrow, loneliness, helpless thoughts. That no one can realise that.

Life is all about, Take your Steps Fast, Before the Count down begins, Take a Coat of your own, Be ready for your turn.

निश्चय करो, आगे बढ़ने की मेहनत सफ़लता का एक ही मंत्र है.....
जीवनकाल एक समंदर है, उछलते लहरों पर जिसका नाव डगमगाया नहीं, जीत उसीका दामन छोड़ कर कभी मुंह मोड़ा नहीं

If your survival in the mother's womb is not so easy...... then how could you think about the whole life????? So let the hard times and bad situations to think again by staring at your beautiful smiling face......

I walked till the end of the road and saw, another turning point is waiting for me, And the journey is "To be Continued"....... And it's called reality of LIFE.

Suhas Prakash Ghoke

Insta id : ghokesuhas

Suhas Prakash Ghoke a passionate writer . From past 3 years he has indulge himself in writings. Right now pursuing a bachelor's degree in the field of Zoology . In love with nature and fond of photography.He is well sounded individual who lives with passion , dedication and grace and want to inspire everyone with his writings.

I trusted you to be there for me yet when the time came when I needed you the most you were the one that pushed me off the ledge . I was only hanging on by a few fingers from. Need to open up now I too have heart to feel, Wanna free yourself in my touch, I'm loosing myself in your eyes of teal, don't give up on me, i love you so much., you're my star, the essence of beauty, I know you've been scarred, but loving you is my duty, let all your fears melt away, loose yourself in my kiss,don't let your feeling sway, let yourself feel this bliss. U say you've already told me all your secrets, But tell me honestly, Do you really love me? You told me so many times that you love me, But do you trust me? To be honest, no words can explain the way I love you, Have I ever I told you? You're the only person I ever said "I love you" I'm broken from the inside; though this heart has had too much to take; with a fake smile on my face; i always try to hide my past mistakes; Having no one to open up to and no one to speak; I can feel the fear and anger within me , I 'm just becoming far too weak. The only reason I have is that i just don't trust anyone , I'm too scared to ask for help; But if I say that I need you !! will you be there for me when i reveal myself? Or will you cut me off from your life just like everybody else do ??? Or just a fake concern?? Can you please just trust me on this .. you're amazing ,different ,worth it, enough you matter and you make a difference . Get it in your head it hurts that you don't see yourself the way I see you....... - Suhas Ghoke . I trusted you to be there for me yet when the time came when I needed you the most you were the one that pushed me off the ledge . I was only hanging on by a few fingers from. Need to open up now I too have heart to feel, Wanna free yourself in my touch, I'm loosing myself in your eyes of teal, don't give up on me, i love you so much., you're my star, the essence of beauty, I know you've been scarred, but loving you is my duty, let all your fears melt away, loose yourself in my kiss,don't let your feeling sway, let yourself feel this bliss. U say you've already told me all your secrets, But tell me honestly, Do you really love me? You told me so many times that you love me, But do you trust me? To be honest, no words can explain the way I love you, Have I ever I told you? You're the only person I ever said "I love you" I'm broken from the inside; though this heart has had too much to take; with a fake smile on my face; i always try to hide my past mistakes; Having no one to open up to and no one to speak; I can feel the fear and anger within me , I 'm just becoming far too weak. The only reason I have is that i just don't trust anyone , I'm too scared to ask for help; But if I say that I need you !! will you be there for me when i reveal myself? Or will you cut me off from your life just like everybody else do ??? Or just a fake concern?? Can you please just trust me on this .. you're amazing ,different ,worth it, enough you matter and you make a difference . Get it in your head it hurts that you don't see yourself the way I see you....... I trusted you to be there for me yet when the time came when I needed you the most you were the one that pushed me off the ledge . I was only hanging on by a few fingers from. Need to open up now I too have heart to feel, Wanna free yourself in my touch, I'm loosing myself in your eyes of teal, don't give up on me, i love you so much., you're my star, the essence of beauty, I know you've been scarred, but loving you is my duty, let all your fears melt away, loose yourself in my kiss,don't let your feeling sway, let yourself feel this bliss. U say you've already told me all your secrets, But tell me honestly, Do you really love me? You told me so many times that you love me, But do you trust me? To be honest, no words can explain the way I love you, Have I ever I told you? You're the only person I ever said "I love you" I'm broken from the inside; though this heart has had too much to take; with a fake smile on my face; i always try to hide my past mistakes; Having no one to open up to and no one to speak; I can feel the fear and anger within me , I 'm just becoming far too weak. The only reason I have is that i just don't trust anyone , I'm too scared to ask for help; But if I say that I need you !! will you be there for me when i reveal myself? Or will you cut me off from your life just like everybody else do ??? Or just a fake concern?? Can you please just trust me on this .. you're amazing ,different ,worth it, enough you matter and you make a difference . Get it in your head it hurts that you don't see yourself the way I see you.......

Tiya Tripathy

Insta id : aesthetics_by_tiya

A banker by profession,an artist by heart☐

Perfectly imperfect

You and I were never meant to be one,
Still my soul keeps yearning for you.
My heart bleeds from my eyes everytime,
I think of the prophecy that's going to be true.

Only on a night so precious like this,
When the sky's emblazed by the blue moon,
We Meet by the brook to find our bliss, Surreptitiously, by a
chance of fortune.

In that one night I live a millenium dreams
Lost in your embrace, drowning in your kiss,
Till the curse of separation moves us apart,
Fading with the moonlight,disappearing without any trace.

Raised in the arms of taboos and superstitions,
The little girl often wondered only if she was a boy,
then she could have been free of all inhibitions,
The thoughts of which filled her little heart with joy.
One day she will be allowed to play till dusk like her brothers
Without worrying about the unwanted apprehensions
That she could choose whatever she liked like the others,
To pave her path of life by changing the directions.
She grew up eventually like a beautiful butterfly,
Only to realise the clasp of restrictions grew tighter,
She wanted to fly away free up in the sky,
And break the stereotypes that surrounded every daughter.
"Girls don't do this, Girls can't do that",
Such remarks made her feel exasperated,
Why was she judged even before trying anything?
To prove her worth, an opportunity she awaited.
Breaking all norms, defying all rules,
She rose one day like the morning sun

And reached to a height has begun.where no one could touch
Declaring the world that a new era

Forged like a weapon of ultimate destruction
She stood above the ground like a corpse revived,
Rising from the ashes of her own incineration
To claim everything that once she deprived.

Haunted by ways she was tormented,
Under the name of laws and salvation
Only was a little freedom she demanded
to lead her life towards emancipation.

She glared at the world with blazing eyes,
disguised as the spirit of vengeance,
No longer could she be kept under leash,
A warrior she was now with no place for tolerance.

Yash Mangalwedhekar

Insta id : yash_mangalwedhekar

A teenage ambivert guy from Maharashtra, who finds ways to express his emotions through words. A nature enthusiast and a romantic writer. Being an overthinker, his happiness lies in making others smile.His addictions include coffee, music and most importantly fitness. @the_soul_words

Write up 1

When you sail high, people will pull you down, On your true success story, they will surely frown. When you crave for help, feeling all alone and low, They will ignore you as always, true colors they will show When you do believe their faces, being innocent and fake, Into a thousand pieces, your trust they will break. When you become famous, the jealousy will be shown, You worked hard, but credits they will own. When you don't listen to them, they'll show you a knife, Don't worry friend, it's the bitter truth of life.

Write up 2

Fed up of love, fed up of life, I need some peace, words cut deeper than knife. Grudges too many, fights too long, I try to make things well, but they take me wrong. I care too much, I just don't know why, End of the day I realize, everything is a lie.

<u>Microtales:</u>

1) Today I visited the place where we used to meet everytime.

I could feel her presence and lingering of her voice around me.

Only then I realised, "life" after death is not a myth.

2)"What were you afraid of?" The boy who attempted sucide was asked.

"Life!" He replied with a heavy voice.

<u>Quote:</u>

1) Life would have been much easier if people stopped expecting from others.

Chahat Sharma

Insta id : @chahatafr1 and @spurting_phrases

Chahat, a blogger, Instagrammer, a writer at 2 news websites, and with her awaited book, is all set to create a change with something the world ignores. She is a strong believer, that- "Words typed are something more influential then the words were spoken".

Birthday's A time when all played music, danced out their night, I preferred staying home. I hated how everyone was calling. No, it was not because I hated them or it was something like a formality. It's just that, birthday's don't make sense to me anymore. With every call I started receiving, I wished they disconnected soon. I don't know why but I hated that night's moon. It was like, why did this date even arrive. Why was it? Why was it all happening? But I had no clue why was I even thinking all this? Was I okay? Well, might be I was just tired. But I did sleep right. So what was it? What is making me get so away from this desirous life? I kept thinking as I took out my laptop and started to type. I received calls from many. Close ones who always wished but there was a lack. That lack was of someone who I truly wanted to be with. I guess I had none that time. And might be this was the reason I wanted to make sure that I stayed all alone, all inside, all away from the crowd. Even lied and disconnected the calls in frustrations a few times. Seemed like what the hell should I talk about? I don't know if we were truly on that same walk. Things were changing, people were the same. I don't know about all but I was not okay. I was just not okay. I disconnected. I took a time out. But what was when I called up again? They said we thought you won't call up. you will ditch us again but did they really ask why? What was going on within? What I lacked inside and what I felt inside? Did they even try to know? Or even if I say, are people even listening? Then what exactly is the birthday's meant for? Just party? Just a celebration? With a fake smile on the face where we throw out parties and serve people with a half-broken smile? Why is it so? Why? Why can't we be normal? Why can't we just live the way we want? We all get broken but why is it that we get broken? Is there anyone who thought about the same as me? I don't know. Might be I would never know. But I will carry around this question all my life because some answers are needed and for me, I am the kind of person who unless given a proper reply, doesn't feel satisfied. I know I will receive it someday. Soon. Thinking all this I slept and slept. The whole day of an important day, how did I spend it? Sleeping. I wasted a complete whole day. woke up had food, went out to meet a friend who called along to have a pastry but why? How many why's we carry around instead?

Finding answers, walking around, thinking from bad to worst, all of the profound.

Sushmita Singh

A jamshedpurian of 22, Sushmita Singh is a student currently pursuing graduation from jamshedpur women's college . She's a student of b.com accounts honours and preparing for bank po exams as well. She aspires to be a writer and an investment banker.Her hobbies are writing novels and literary fiction books. She has been a part of various anthologies as co-author and compiler as well . She dreams to pocket everything she could and would.

Tears,sorrows,unhappiness surrounds me
Apart from the goods I have done to many
Still this loneliness and isolation holds me tightly...
I shiver in the darkest moments of my life
Those moments which breaked me and turned me stone...
Being crowded with people I still feel alone

Clearing my cupboard, I saw my old turtleneck...(sweater)
A sudden smile was welcomed by my face...
I held it smelled it
However it carried the same smell
Smell of my innocence, even after many years...
The smell which I inherit no more...

I still have those Beautiful memories captured through ur camera...
The efforts you made to bring them altogether locked up with all ur
love in that magnification photo frame...
But still my heart wishes the efforts you had put capturing those
moments
Could possibly get u back...

The scratches, her scars were telling her story ....
But the pain was much deeper inside...
The ideology of society was not affecting her
But the tears of her parents, killed her
She almost lost everything
But in that blaming crowd , he still held her hand firmly
And in this harsh reality of life
The miracle happened to her
No wonder that was true love

From being a girl next door
To being the hell goddess
I burnt the sweet one inside me
Cause I'm no more interested to behave like someone modest
You may judge me and I know
I possibly don't care what you think of me
And it doesn't effect me anymore
That sweetness filled up smiles left my lips long ago
Long ago enough to forget
All started and ended as I was taken up as an easy target
Dont even trynna giving me your sympathetic advice
I'm still the unbreakable even if he was my bad choice...

Suyog Mainali

Born in 1998 in Kathmandu, Nepal is a proud Nepalese citizen who lives in India to complete his education.

Writing didn't start early in his life as he just begun writing poems in a diary just to tear and throw them away at the age of 13 and when he reached 19 that is at 2017 his friends inspired him to publish his work. So, he started posting poems on instagram at his page named thepoeticsensation. That's from where he has been discovered.

He writes about life as a whole but he specialises in writing about recently occurred events.

<u>Acid</u>

You've been throwing acid
When she declined your love
You say that you are placid
And that you act as a dove

Now justify your actions
All the mayhem that you caused
The beautiful little girl
Is suffering for no cause

Now she's on a bed
Thinking what wrong had she done
When you motherfucker
Think you have done nothing wrong

What can I say
You've flee from the scene
Only one of three caught
After killing her dreams

<u>Late Night</u>

It's late night and she's walking down the streets
In the clothes she feels
All she had was good vibes
She's going to touch the sky she is unstoppable

In the dark was no knight in a shining armour
But four guys with bad intentions

Whistling and hooting as the girl passes by
Licking their lips with horny temptations

Fuck their values they attacked her like a hound
Grabbed her by the waist to pull her to the earth
She starts screaming and crying out loud
But her efforts were of no avail

She is now broken too afraid to call the cops
Overthinking that her name will come out
Being raped she thinks her motive in life is lost
And starts thinking about the thoughts of the crowd

Now she stays all day locked in her room
I don't understand stand why
She regrets to have blessed her mother's womb
And decides to take her own life

Welcome to Earth

Hello welcome to Earth, I will be serving for you today

Can I take your order, yes please thank you

I would love a plate of negativity for the starter

And would love to look at the menu

So, let's order a drink it's called shake of lies

With a topping of sarcasm would be pretty nice

And can you change the song and start a fight

Then only I enjoy war as the veggies to my rice

Thank you for your order and here are foods

Wow the food is served in an arsenal it looks beautiful

But I would like some gunpowder you might have forgot to put

You'd have gotten a five star rating if you served like it should

SAKET SINGH

I am a Mechanical engineer. I belongs to Bihar and completed basic studies from
Ranchi. I write poetry and motivational stories.

<u>Life in Summer vacation</u>

Life was roughly smooth,

Then comes summer vacation.

Vacation for young children

And untold pressure to elder one.

Teachers think for other options,

they need money to feed family.

They feel deserted ,

While others have fun time.

Some school's owner get frightened

Since students tend to change

the school and environment.

Students feel free at home,

Teachers get stuck in situation,

finding way to feel at home.

To some people and businesses,

This vacation is time

to work and enhance

the possibility of outcome,

And only time to earn

and feed the family

till next season.

The harsh life in hot summer,

Seems cool to their hard living,

But just as some droplets

Sprinkled on a frying pan.

The time for development

and the time of decay,

together makes the statistics figure

anonymously equivalent to and

at equilibrium, the analyst says.

Mohammad Saifuddin

19 years old, born in Madhupur a sub-division of dist-Deoghar, Jharkhand. Indulged in poetry since 8 years though pursued BSc in Mathematics. Trying to convey the idea of universal humanity and Love as the ultimate goal of mankind.

A Dream

A mistress full quite quaint,
New as flower and pure as saint.
A melody flows through the eyes of her
And her tongue pours some heavenly liqu'r.

A castle at the top of mount Helicon,
From where the magical river flows. Beside which is the
Hippocrene
Cherished her with adorning sheen.

Warrior dancing to maketh her smile,
And fairies uttering most euphonic sound.
Horsemen did march to give her shield,
Chirping birds with dragons prowling around.

A valiant didst did cross by the woods,
Ceased by the lake and satteth on a stone.
Wast in search of some honey to drink,
Writing the rhyme of life with stainless ink.

The eyes didst did match and it rained,
Stainless ink wast deeply stained.
Heart didst did seize seeing the fearless dove,
Once who wast a warrior hast fallen in love.

In scarlet cheeks were not for shame,
Loving her wast though a censured blame.
That gent did rush her festinate and did kiss her cheek,
Did hold her hand and I did wake up again.

The Proposal

Wouldst thee believe if it be true I say,
If I say mine own eyes find a child in thee.
If it be true I say these eyes has't ceased looking,
Ever since those gents has't seen thee.

Wouldst thee believe if it be true I say
I hath heard while gath'ring may.
Flowers gossip'd about thee,
Their petals nay softer than ye.

If it be true I say mine own ears ceased hearing,
Ever since those gents has't heard thee.
If it be true I say thee truly art mine own life, lief
Coequal though this wilt not beest true.

If it be true this beest a poetry and I doth loveth thee,
Mine own heart yells, I loveth thee true.

The Peddle

The peddle of disdain is a foul for sure,
As yond wast his loveth fair and pure.
The light wast nay doubt a part of him,
As he hast chosen darkness for to cure.

Death did pity him and eyes did cry,
It was a rain when no drop did lie.
Vail of a melodious rhyme was sung,
Yodelling thine voice was fair and shy.
Amidst the hustle wast thine fairest song.

Yond hath led to felony of loveless heart,
And led to the agony of heartless bird.
Art did witness it's downfall, lief mate;
Roads not chosen were all exsufflicate.
As pain danced in whose melody was a poet.

Shibangi das

A girl with full of mess and a hell lot of confusion, has immense love for zoology, recently at her 2nd yr in graduation
A bookaholic ambivert
Life seems a puzzle to her and writing is helping her to solve it.
Writing is hobby-turned-passion for her and she aims to change the society with her inkings

LEFTOVER

Ask a poor child
Who is hungry for days
How delicious leftover food is to him.
Ask an old man
Shivering in the cold nights
How much warmth
A blanket tore apart gave to him
Ask a thirsty
How sufficient a drop of water
Adhered to the base of a glass
To quench his thirst.

Leftovers are waste
Isn't it what we think?
But then,
Every coin has two sides
Is that not what we say?

IMPERFECTIONS AND FAULTS

I wish I could erase the past
to mend my innumerable faults
to mend the broken hearts
injured by unfulfilled expectations,
I wish I could fulfil
those unfulfilments.
But then
what is a life
without flaws

How would we know
the value of being right
in the absence of wrongs?
Mistakes are necessary
Imperfections are fine
Flaws are great
So now i wish
to lose the eraser
that could erase the past
and to never find it.

A POETIC ADVICE

Whenever experiencing
A bite of bitter memories
Hurting you
Piercing into your flesh
Let it do
More deeper the wound
The more you arouse
Your inner sense gets alarmed
Of not repeating those mistakes
Of not lamenting over
Of your victory coming its way
Over inner demonic thoughts
Let it be there
For erasing it
 won't make you better
That spotted wound only
Will make you greater

Lasika Chapdi

Myself lasika Chapdi... Love bringing smile in everyone's face.....
Friends call me little psychologist.... Writing is not only my hobby
but it's my life..

<u>Write up 1</u>

Are you not trying in fear of becoming a failure? Remember your trial may result as failure..... But winner are those who never lose hope.... And real failure are the ones those who don't try or end's up by becoming failure..... Make a cycle Learn, try, focus, fail Failure, Focus on mistake, improve, try again and be a winner!!

<u>Write up 2</u>

Hyy you yes you!!! Don't be worried..... Be positive and..... Let everything alright

<u>Write up 3</u>

117

Leaves of Tress makes me believe.... Losing doesn't means end....
Giving doesn't means take..... Leaving doesn't need friends.....
Even though important for livings But did really anyone care!!!
Shade shadow for people to rest.... Even people doesn't cares.....
Tree's are important for everyone!!! Did you ever thought of
growing tree's? It's okk you are thinking of better today! But what's
about you

are growing worst tomorrow.... Suffering from deforestation!!!
Will future can be alive? Plant a tree.... For your young once to
survive!!!

Akshita Gautam

I am Akshita from Patna. Writing is my passion

Write up 1

I have many friends Who absolved my fruitless bends A dearth of happiness in this world Is what they easily lends But all these friendship seems so insignificant in night Slightly bemused, that golden star is moving towards end With an infinite horizon of darkness Around its space Forlorn on a ghastly base. The golden star looks faded, inspite of seeing the rays of sun, it was impossible to chase The immutable had to change its race Then, it gave births to new impeccable stars The world whom admires its grace The star lamented over the lost sun Bravery is what you need to be that "Never ending pace"

Write up 2

She has a charisma of ethical personality fuelled with the sublime colours of perpetual euphoria. I love you. I love you when your wrinkles of skin sparks for me, When you tries to be flamboyant sea, When your hands work day and night, When you show the strange passion to fight. I love you even when you are flickering light Cause you are my only sight The thread of my flying kite. I love you when you surreptitiously love me When you make me carefree Being the deep root of my verdant tree You always behaved with utmost propriety. I love the way you walk the way you talk the way you care the way you share.. In my myriad dreams you r the best personality In love with your creation and obliterate ability. The presence of yours Seems so true and cures The crevices in the walls of life Clears the ambiguous road of success Heals the pain of burnt face.. You are so good and facile The repentance in me comes for a while Sometimes i disparage you

<u>Write up 3</u>

STORMS Let it tear u apart Cause it teaches u more than art U can run out in fear Or take the responsibility to make things clear The dark clouds striking lurid details Restructuring the horrible tales. U can swallow the pain Or try to escape a single drop of rain. The path full of grief But triumph must b ur belief U can face the infinity Touch the untraceable heights A man of Sanctity Try to win the toughest fights....

S.Manaswitha

Manaswitha Sambareddy
Vijayawada, A.P
Age 18
Mandala art and calligraphy are the major hobbies
Loves to cook...foodie...

Mistakes are made.. to be done in past to make you perfect in future. So,Don't use eraser to bring back the pastpencil to present, better to make a pastpen. But still...if you are thinking about a peneraser in future..No one minds of you, not the mistake.

Somethings never change....

From my bedroom window
to next door aunty's balcony
 the way she looks and
 the complaints she give

Somethings never change....

From 99 missed calls by mom
To 1 missed call by 'aunty' in friends phone
From "Did u eat ?"
To "did she/he eat ?"

Somethings never change....

From "Need a pencil dady"
To " Macha...2b pencil da.."
From "anna...where is my small scale......."
To " Macha..return my L scale da.."

Somethings never change....

From "Amma....A4 sheet for project..."
To " deyyy....one butter sheet da.."
From" appa...print out"
To " macha... trace it da..."

Somethings never change....

SOMETHINGS never change....

Minds getting locked in the curves in
Melting hearts of rock
Made from the brush in his hand,
Manufactured in a pure soul.
Mastering the imaginations with
Marvellous creative skills in
Making the word beautiful to most..
Mesmerized big black eyes and
Memorable long hair
Moments with the red beak
Meaning to a complete telugu girl
Meaning of friendship....Bapuramana

Mother to tears
How much is your pain....
Tears said ocean depth....

Tears to mother
How much is.. your pain...
When my baby cry, but still I smile...

One, two , three,...
Just a number

Marks we score...
Just a number

Degrees we get...
Just a number

Money we earn...
Just a number

Limits we have...
Just a number

Age we grow...
Just a number...

Time we pass...
Just a number,
But never REPEATs...

People we meet...
Stories we listen...

Distance we travel...
Places we go...

Books we read...
Pages we turn...

Problems we met...
Lessons we learnt...

More we Explore...
More we Explode...

Two little small silver anklets....
Making a sound galgalgal...
Running to the gates that are opened by hearts..
Shouting mamamahh...
Asking 'where are my festival laddus?'...
Where other iron voice..
A bit rusted...Shouts...
Who is this mental girl?...we don't know you..

Asking that little red chilli...
Again and again...
To listen her sweet voice...

And that little dhorasaani says...manasheetha....

-S.Manaswitha